VIKAAR

SANKALP SINGH PAL

Acknowledgements

Writing Vikaar has been a journey of exploration, patience, and growth — a journey that would not have been possible without the unwavering support and inspiration of some incredible people.

First and foremost, my wife, Bhagyashree, whose love, understanding, and steadfast support have been the foundation on which this book stands. Your feedbacks and unbiased reviews have made this story waht it is. Your faith in me, even when I doubted myself, has been my greatest source of motivation.

A very special and deepest gratitude to Shraddha and Vishnu. Your encouragement, insightful discussions, and belief in this project gave me the strength to move forward even during the most challenging moments

To all the readers who provided their guidance and feedback along the way — thank you for helping me shape Vikaar into what it has become. Every word written carries a piece of your kindness, wisdom, and belief.

With heartfelt gratitude,
Sankalp Singh Pal

I SHALL NOT WALK FREE

Heavy footsteps, from the outer premises of the police headquarters, New Delhi, walking down the busy corridors of the HQ, made their way swiftly and intently to the person behind a desk who was wrapping up for the day. Down a huge hall, swiftly up the staircase, a left and a right led the file bearer to a person who was being sacked, who had spent the last five months trying to convince his bosses to reconsider him and give him a second chance. But all his requests, his begging, his aggression, his glorious service records, and even cries of his visibly declining mental and physical health fell on deaf ears and closed doors. He was Dr. Raman Sharma.

A file smashes on his desk. "You wanted a second chance? Here it is." He sniffed something and continued, "And when was the last time you took a shower?" The recipient was not perplexed, but surely, this snapped him out of his mental slumber, which he had induced since the demise of his wife. He saw a man standing in front of him, disgusted by Raman's sheer appearance, and wondering what had made their superiors give him such an important case. He saw the file bearer leaving the room with an utterly blank expression. He picked up the file and flipped open the leaflet,

Name – Sarvadaman Singh, Age – 28 years, Height – 6'0, Weight – 91 kgs, Skin Colour – Dusky, Accused of – Torture and Murder of Bhavesh Raina.

The sheer sight of the case details bored him, which was evident from the expressions on his face. His eyebrows were slightly tensed, and he was trying hard to keep his eyes open. There were wrinkles on his forehead in an attempt to keep this expression, fine lines on the corners of his eyes, and nothing changed shape. His face sat flat with no interest in this world. His heartbeat was slow and composed as normal. He kept the file back on the desk and left. At twenty three hundred hours, his phone rang. "Interesting enough?" the voice on the other side of the phone asked. He replied with a sniff and a smirk on his face, "It has been over a year since I have tried to reach you, literally asking you, begging for help to keep myself sane, but this is how you say sorry! By giving me the most plain, and ill-tasting case. A murder case! A homicide where you have already caught the guy. Sir, if you did not want to entertain my requests, why even go through the trouble of sending the file over?"

The voice on the other side of the phone continued, "I thought so. But you will have to bear this. Go meet him…" Raman interrupted, "Meet him! Seriously! You think I will meet him? Which word of mine told you that I am interested? Are you not listening? I am not going to waste my time talking to some random, amateur killer." The voice continued, "Go and meet him once, then I will leave it up to you, if you want the case or not. Tomorrow, at nine hundred hours, we leave for Bangalore." The voice responded to his disgust. "What! Bangalore? Nine o'clock? Are you kidding me?" Raman kept shouting at his phone, not knowing that there was no one on the other side. "Hello, hello, hello!" he shouted in utter frustration.

He was mentally prepared to turn down the offer, so he reached the airport by 7:30 AM. Looking at hordes of people in the bustling metropolis, trying to reach somewhere and thinking, that by walking, sitting, talking to unknown and complete strangers, none of them has the faintest idea of what mask the other person is wearing. The façade they uphold to hide their true instincts. All the mannerism, the politeness, the cleanliness, all to lure in the petty and vulnerable people, and at the exact right time, they open their malicious jaws to devour innocence."

A man came and sat beside him, handing over a boarding pass. He panned his vision with a little jerk and shock. "All the arrangements are done, you need not worry about anything," said the man with a thick white beard, and a corporate suit that sat on his heavy build; the sharpness of an eagle was evident from behind the shades. The gait of a tiger, the elegance of a lion, and the agility of a jaguar were still visible from his old frame. He further continued, "On landing, you will be escorted to the Central Jail. Tell them that I sent you. They will fill you in on the rest of the information." A car came and stopped in front of them. The suited man got up and boarded the car, and before it drove off, he said, "I take care of the men who are useful."

Raman sat there in absolute awe of the man. He had a lot on his mind; at least a hundred reasons to say no. But the sheer aura of the person who had just left, made it impossible for him to even ask questions, let alone reject the proposal. But somewhere, in some deep corner of his mind and heart, he was craving for a hunt. He had no other option but to comply with the orders. But also, to quench his bloodlust. He got up and made his way to board the plane.

Upon landing at Kempegowda International Airport, he saw a constable with a placard with "Dr. Raman Sharma Sir" written on it. Raman made his way to the constable. The poor policeman had no clue who he was waiting for. He was getting anxious about how his guest looked and who was making his way towards him now and demanding his attention. He took a look at Raman, and after slight hesitation and confusion, he drew a photograph from his pocket, trying to match the facial features of the man standing in front of him.

Raman understood that the constable was at a total loss at this labour of his, so he removed his goggles in an attempt to help the poor policeman. "Oh! Sir, Sorry, I did not realise, Sir! It was you. You look different, very different from the photo." With an awkward giggle, he flipped the photograph to prove his case. "Yeah, this was me when I was in the academy." Raman explained, suddenly amidst his clarification, "Oh! Head Constable Shaktivel, Sir."

The constable saluted him with a sharp thump of the foot and a sharp hand gesture. Raman replied, "It's not necessary. I am not an officer." To which Shaktivel replied, "You must be someone important, otherwise Jailer *saab* would not be so excited for your arrival." He led Raman to a police car and they both left for the prison. Their three-hour drive was largely composed of silence and regular checks of "Tea, sir? Coffee?" to which Raman denied. The calm and cool winds of the city and the warmth of the glimmering sun of the early hours of the day gave Raman a much-needed and coveted comfort and cosiness, which made him slip into slumber.

The outer roads of the city were smooth enough to help him transition from conscious to the subconscious realm. He gradually felt that someone was sitting beside him. Before he could turn to see who it was, two hands with a firm yet soft and familiar grip curled around his left arm. And before he could register what had just happened, a head came and rested on his left shoulder. He turned around and saw Aditi!

Resting her head upon his shoulder, and clasping his palm between her knees. "Isn't the weather superb?" It had been so long that he had heard her voice, let alone respond to it. But somehow he knew what he was about to say, as if he had had this conversation before. "It is, and you make it even more pleasant." Aditi then replied, "Give some credit to yourself, Dr. Raman. What a master stroke you have played. I kept complaining about you not giving me surprises, taking me out, and all. But you! In a single clean swipe, did it all."

Then suddenly he sees a large mob of people in front of the car, which causes the driver to slow down the car. The mob was led by a huge, burly man with his mouth covered with a muffler. He made his way swiftly to an almost-stopped car, opened the gate on Raman's side, and asked him to get out. Raman was startled and did not understand the reason behind his demand. He tried to scoot back in the seat to create a room between him and the unknown intruder. But the man started being more and more assertive, to the point where he grabbed Raman's right shoulder and shook it. This action confused Raman, as it was not threatening. Then he heard a high-pitched voice, "Wake up, sir, we have reached, sir."

Raman opened his eyes and found himself in the compound of the Central Jail, and Shaktivel was trying to wake him up. Upon reaching the prison, Shaktivel escorted Raman to the jailer's office. He gestured for him to sit on the bench kept right outside the office. One other man was sitting beside him; he was cuffed to the bench. The stranger sat back, blankly looking to his side, despite many people and other things to set one's gaze on. Yet it felt as if he was staring deep into something! His stillness sent chills down Raman's spine.

The air around him was crawling with silence yet chaos. Every blink of his eyes was deep and profound like they were surfing on each ripple of time. A pair of specs sitting on his nose gave him a serious appearance. There was nothing unusual about him, yet he was there and cuffed. It was clear that he had committed a crime, grave enough to be handcuffed and made to sit here. But his open body language, with legs apart, relaxed shoulders, and chest out, and regular and slow breathing, showed that he knew that he would walk away free from here and that there was a mistake on the system's side.

I was still curious and was about to initiate a conversation right then. Raman was called in. The jailer welcomed him, and after formalities, he started explaining the scenario. "The case is not usually complicated, you see. We have a victim, we have a 'who', we have a 'when', and fascinatingly, we have a 'where'. It was so easy, he did not even try to hide it. He didn't even try to escape. But what I am interested in is 'why', which we do not have. He just refuses to speak whenever it comes to it.

The evidence is conclusive enough to prove him guilty, but the government lawyer who took his case will try hard to prove that he is mentally unfit, which might allow him to walk away without any repercussions. I don't want that! I don't want him to see the sun again. That's why you are here. To rule out any possibility of mental illness that might help him in any way." The jailer said and continued, "I hope you have already gone through the file and other details that we sent?" referring to the case file that Raman had brought with him. The jailer continued, "I will not bore you by telling what you already know. So, Dr. Raman, he is all yours. All we don't want is, him walking away free."

Raman replied, "I will do my best to help you in whichever way possible, and I also assure you that he will not walk free *if proven guilty!*" Raman's eyes glowed with a rebellious fire. He then said, "By the way, where is he... Sarvadaman Singh." The jailer looked confused by his question. Jailer replied, "I believe you have already met him." To which Raman replied with a question mark on his face, which was answered by a full stop of the jailer's finger pointing towards the door where he saw a man, sitting, looking blankly towards his side, but somehow aware that he was being looked at; then he suddenly turned and stared right back at them. A chill ran down Raman's spine, who hadn't felt such a sensation in years.

Raman walked towards the bench. "Sarvadaman?" and as if he was pulled out of deep meditation, he scanned Raman from top to bottom and saw the jailer and Shaktivel standing in the background. "Can we talk somewhere in the open, where there are not many people? I don't like closed rooms, I am claustrophobic," said Sarvadaman. Raman felt a deep innocence in his eyes and a firm stillness in his voice. He looked at the jailer hopefully and asked if this could be arranged. Jailer nodded in affirmation and ordered Shaktivel to make the necessary arrangements. It took them some time to make the necessary setup for interrogation. A wooden desk with a metallic hook bolted atop it was kept with chairs on both sides in a secluded courtyard of the prison. Anyone's access was restricted in that part of the compound for the time the interrogation would happen. The number of guards was reduced to a mere ten.

Then, Sarvadaman was brought in. He looked nothing like a criminal, far from someone to be brought to such a high-security prison. He was proud in his walk yet polite with his body language, as if he knew the future, and all this was just a futile effort of trying to evade the inevitable. He was seated opposite Raman. His hands which were cuffed together till now were then cuffed to the bolt on the desk. Shaktivel stood at a certain distance, beside the jailer.

Once they thought that everything was right, the jailer gestured for Raman to start. "Hi, I am Dr. Raman Sharma, Criminal Psychologist with the department. I help by profiling the suspects, helping them to establish any possibility of a psychosys at hand, or, like this case, eliminate the possibility of any mental illness. So be free and do not hold back on any information while answering my questions, as I might be the last man standing between you and certain death." Sarvadaman heard everything and responded, "Dr. Raman, I am Sarvadaman Singh. I am from Rajasthan, working here as an employee of an esteemed conglomerate. I am married. My wife's name is Pratigya Singh. It has been 3 years since we were in wedlock and 9 months, 3 weeks, and 4 days since she went missing. I hope this all checks out from the file I assume you have read a couple of times by now. So, shall we move on to the important part?"

He was sharp and confident in his answers. Raman pretended to cross-check his statements and be disinterested. A bias started to creep in. Raman was not a police officer, but a mind specialist. He could feel the pain Sarvadaman was in, behind his composed façade. Raman prepared himself to ask the next set of questions and flipped a paper to see the details of the murder. As Sarvadaman rightly said, this was not the first time Raman read the file, still a drop of sweat rolled down from his temple to his neck and around the Adam's apple before getting devoured by the cuff of his shirt, which Raman used to wipe off. The sheer brutality of a murder showed that Sarvadaman enjoyed doing all of that. Which most psycho killers do, during prolonged periods of torture that they inflict on their victims. But there was also the fact that most psychos have a really tough time fitting into society. But Sarvadaman seems to be a perfectly normal guy with no clue that he is capable of such extreme violence.

Actually, it's not violence itself that gives you that gut-wrenching feeling. It's the feeling that you get when the blade of a knife cuts through the skin, or when a nail leaves the skin when pulled by pliers, or the sheer shivering of the victim's body trying to minimise the trauma. That's what keeps the wild side submerged under waves of time. But this case seems different; this seems like a crack in his mould that made his whole personality collapse and wash away to leave no trace, so there is no reason for him to contain anything.

Raman looked at Sarvadaman, who had a look of concern on his face. He understood what Raman had in his mind. "Yes, I did that to him, and I had every reason for it. But I will only tell you if you promise me that you will hear my story without interrupting me." Raman had no option but to agree as he was intrigued and felt a rush of anticipation. Sarvadamam started right off, "Pratigya and I were introduced by a common friend, her childhood friend, who worked with me. We were instantly attracted to each other. I, being an introvert, was not able to make eye contact with her. But also could not stand a second if she wasn't around. She filled the atmosphere with such an electrifying energy that it made me restless. She blew my mind every time my sight caught hold of her.

Even if it meant from one high to another, I wanted to be in her presence. I started finding excuses to meet her. And every time we met, it was like me rediscovering myself, and every time she left, she left me drained and high on endorphins. Everything stated appeared pink. Music in my head did not stop from the day I saw her. For the first time in my life, I was not living it, I was flowing with it. There were weeks when I could not get to see her because of her engagements somewhere. Sometimes there were weekends that seemed too short, for listening to her random stories. It was all going great till that night when I was having a coffee at a nearby café and was on a call with a friend. Talking about…. Well, something boys talk about.

Clearly, unaware. I got up from a chair, and on my way out, I heard a giggle that timed perfectly with something I said. On further enquiry, I found a woman sitting right behind where I was seated just a few seconds ago. It was Pratigya who had overheard my conversation and found bits of it amusing. My legs were weakened by the sight of her. It was the first time since our introduction that we were facing each other alone. My heart was racing, pumping too much blood in my brain, as I could see everything in slow motion. She giggled, hidden behind the cup of coffee, held between her palms. Her slowly rising eyes, and keeping the cup on the desk seemed like a minute-long piece of cinema.Though hesitant, I stayed back. We sat and talked for hours.

The first time my concentration broke from her smile and big eyes was when the bulb hanging over our table went on. We were talking for hours. We ordered dinner and then went for a walk. The night grew darker, so we exchanged numbers and kept talking till four in the morning. At last, she texted, 'I think we should try to get some sleep now. Luckily, it is still Sunday.' To which I replied with 'Yes. Of course,' with a heavy heart. The next few minutes were silent, and I was surfing on waves of my imagination.

Right then, I got a text from Pratigya, "I really enjoyed my day. We should definitely do this more often. And we don't need Mukta every time we go out." It was then that I realised that this is what we both want. Each other's company! We started going out together. This became our daily ritual. We started ditching group outings and hiding our weekend plans. Never before in my life has a four-and-a-half-hour sleep felt sufficient, and walking into the office at 9 AM never felt early.

Mornings were not good without her text, and dreams were not sweet without her in them. Not long after that, I confessed my feelings to her. It took me a good week to plan every move and word. It felt equally difficult to talk to her, just like the first day I met her. My legs were weak, breathing heavy, and my arms were limp. And my soul almost left my body when I confessed to her about how I felt about her. But to my surprise, even she wanted this to happen. I was the happiest man on earth that day. After that, the next logical step was to tie the knot of holy matrimony. We hoped to live happily ever after. We had every reason to think so. We loved each other; we loved each other's company. But destiny had a trick up its sleeve for us. One day, we came across Bhavesh. Mukta's new boyfriend. They make a dynamic power couple, successful in the sense of the city's vocabulary and riding on the wave of the city's pop culture, who are living their lives to the fullest. They spent every night as their last on earth, and every weekend was a new location and a party that took them to a different realm. Pratigya and Mukta were childhood friends.

That's when I learnt that Bhavesh and Mukta met at one such weekend party, which was high in every sense. And after some casual outings and fooling around, they were together. Bhavesh did not have conventional employment. But had a very lavish and flamboyant lifestyle. He had a brass neck. He didn't think about what he was saying or to whom. Sometimes his behaviour left me offended and wonderstruck, but I did not say anything as I thought this is how people talk. Yet life was fun, and it was they who introduced me to this glittering side of the city, and though it attracted me, it could not engulf us as everyone else around.

One night we had to stay back at Mukta's place as both of them were sloshed. I helped Bhavesh to bed, and Pratigya did the same for Mukta. 'I think I will stay with her tonight if she gets up, and Bhavesh is of no help. I will take the couch here,' Pratigya insisted. I agreed and took the bed in the room beside me. It was not much past 3 AM when Pratigya came and curled up next to me. I hugged her tightly and realised she was sobbing. I asked her about the matter, but she did not say anything. I was too tired to investigate further; hence, I presumed it must have been a nightmare, so I went back to sleep. She woke me up at five, 'I think we should leave,' she said. 'Yeah. Are they awake?' I asked. 'No, but I have to reach the office early, so it would be good to start and reach home when there is no traffic,' she elaborated.

We left their place, but for the whole way home, she did not say anything. I assumed it was the late-night effect, hence I stayed silent. But since then, she seemed unusually quiet, almost lost, and paranoid at all times. She also made sure to maintain distance while sleeping, and even if by mistake, my hand would touch her in sleep, she would violently wake up and mend the border between us. She was only a shadow of herself after that night. I tried to get through the barrier she had created around her by trying to take her out. But she just denied every plan, especially if it was with Mukta. I even tried asking Mukta for help, but it only worsened the situation. It was high time I figured out what was troubling her. One day, I decided to confront her about this. She burst into tears and kept crying for the next three hours. She told me that night, when we stayed at Mukta's, Bhavesh got up in the middle of the night when she was in the bathroom, cornered her outside the bathroom, pushed her in, and tried to force himself on her. She could not understand what had gotten into him, but every time she tried to push harder or scream,

Bhavesh would cover her mouth or choke her. And since then, he has been turning up everywhere she was alone, and in an attempt to apologise for what he did under the effect of alcohol, he, at multiple times, touched and grabbed her inappropriately. I could not believe my ears! I could not comprehend that she was dealing with all this, and I was not there for her. I was enraged and…"

Raman interrupted him, "So you killed him. But why in such a way?" Sarvadaman continued, "I told you not to interrupt me. This is your last chance, doctor," and continued once he was sure that Raman would not interrupt again. "I got up furiously to confront Bhavesh and Mukta about this and beat the hell out of that pervert, but Pratigya held my hand, begging me not to react as it would bring shame to us, and no one would say anything to him as he was drunk and out of his senses.

Why couldn't we leave them alone, and why didn't I do anything then? Why so late? I was not convinced by her argument and tried to convince her to report Bhavesh to the police, but she kept pleading to let this go and maintain distance from them. I eventually caved in, seeing her helpless. I regret this decision of mine now!

From that day, we avoided every possible outing with them and limited our interactions from the bare minimum to a need-to-do basis. And even if we had to be in a place with them, I made sure Pratigya was not alone even for a minute. But a few months later, I had to be out of town for two weeks. We did not stress about it as this was not the first time I was gone, and also we avoided and ignored Bhavesh and Mukta and kept our interactions to the bare minimum for close to a year now. This was my biggest mistake. I was in constant contact with Pratigya to make sure she was okay. But five days later, I got a call from Mukta, she asked me to return as early as possible, cause Pratigya had gone missing. My stomach sank to the floor. I collapsed. Somehow, I managed to make my way back.

I went straight to the police station and enquired what had happened. Officers handled the situation calmly in spite of my being in a frenzy. They told me that our friends Mukta and Bhavesh went to our home, but found no one there. When they called Pratigya on her mobile, they did not get any answer from the other side. They waited for a while, but seeing no sign of her return, they enquired about her whereabouts with the neighbours. They came to know that no one had seen her out of the house lately, and especially not at all in the last two days. They smelled something fishy and reached out to the police. It was then that I got a call from Mukta asking me to return.

I was sent home, assured that the police were looking for my wife and would contact me if there was a new finding. I could not differentiate reality from fiction as it all seemed a bizarre nightmare. Bhavesh and Mukta came to my home later that evening. And after spending a few hours trying to console me and fixing me with dinner, they left. But Bhavesh was behaving strangely. It was my prejudice against him that could have made me think like that, so I quickly flushed this thought from my mind, and anyway, if he had done anything, why would he involve the police?

The next few days went by going to the station and returning empty-handed. It sucked the soul of my body. One evening Bhavesh called me and asked me if I would care to join them for an outing with a couple of other friends. I said no at first, but then he invited himself over to my house. I was in no state of mind for a house party, so I agreed to join them. It was him, me, and another couple. We were talking about things that were none of my concern. I never enjoyed such ambience and company and with Pratigya not there and not just that, not knowing where she was made it even more unbearable for me.

So, I excused myself from the conversation and pretended to visit the loo, trying to evade the nonsense conversation the other three were having. It was on my way back that I ventured into the bathroom and heard it all. 'He has gone mad, about his wife being missing. I hope you have done what you were supposed to, as you have been rewarded handsomely. I do not want any loose ends, it's not the first time you have done it, but this time, I am way too close to fire." He then waited for a few seconds and then said what seemed to be a reply. "You have no business in knowing whose body is that. You just have to take care of it like others before this. And being your benevolent benefactor, I assume you will not make a mess this time."

He again stopped and then again said with a more relaxed voice. "Yes, she is. And her husband is acting weird. I mean, who wants to get stuck with one person for their whole life? It's like digging the same hole over and over, where's the fun in that? But I also don't blame him. Even I would love to dig that hole again and again.' And then he smirked and laughed. He further said, 'I definitely am and love my wife too. But who said loyalty and love have to be mutually exclusive? If I am not happy, how can I keep her happy? Mukta likes trying new things, so I have to learn them and practice them multiple times before I finally give her the treat. And man-o-man! that Pratigya…'

My ears went erect. 'She was something else. Her dusky skin felt like butter and certainly tasted like wine. Her body was thick in perfect proportions and had enough to scoop from. The smell of her body sent chills down my spine. Her limbs seemed as if they would melt under the application of force. When I pulled her towards my bare chest, I could feel her muslin soft skin. Her body was so warm and soft, just like butter. But she was not easy to control. She was strong! It was very hard to control her. She even tried to hurt me by scratching, punching, and kicking, but every time she lost her balance or tried to take off, I ripped off a piece of her clothes.

Firstly, the sleeves of her *kurti*, when she tried to push me away. Then a piece of cloth from her back, when she kicked the wall against which I held her. It exposed her back to her waist. Her skin colour was glittery with sweat and shone like copper. It shrouded my mind with lust. I could not wait anymore to see what was beneath the rest of her clothes. But every time I tried, she would not let me. So I slapped her real hard. She fell to the ground and was disoriented. I then held her by her hand and pulled her to the bed, where I had kept those silky ropes that I was about to try that night on Mukta, as a gift on her return. One by one, I tied her arms and legs to the bedpost. Then I started unwrapping my gift slowly. Her vigorous movement made it difficult for me to focus on anything else but her perfectly busty chest. When I got every piece of cloth off of her.

My jaw dropped. It was the most perfectly sculpted body I had ever seen. There was no black spot on her body, except those patches on her meaty and absolutely round chest. I don't even know how hard I bit them while feeling the rest of her body with my hands, but she screamed loudly as if she wanted me to continue. She was tight! From everywhere, top to bottom. Her arms, her belly, her chest, her thighs. Her puffy modesty lay there uncovered as if it had never been touched. It called me. I squeezed her chest and her body. The sweat added to her flavour, which felt like chocolate syrup. I started smelling and licking her violently and rapidly. But could not get enough.

I started rubbing between her legs with my two fingers, and after a while, they were wet. I licked all the juices oozing from her hole. It smelled like roses and tasted like salted caramel. It was overwhelming for me. I had not seen anything like this ever before. Even her armpits smelled like ocean mist.

I never thought I would feel my tool so tight ever again. Then I thought of entering her. I pulled out my meat and put her moist modesty. She had clenched it but gave up in some moments. I made a quick move and pushed myself in. The warmth and moisture inside took me to a new high that I had never experienced. Then once! Twice! And then three more times, I emptied myself into her. Her crying and resistance had stopped by the third time. Only tears rolled down her face, which motivated me to please her more. So, I sat cleaning the area between her legs that were pulled wide apart, using my tongue. It felt like coffee-flavoured maple sauce. Ufff...... I am getting wet just thinking about that night. Her crying felt like a symphony.

We could have had so much fun behind Sarvadaman and Mukta's backs, but she had to ruin all the fun by trying to escape. The knot on one of her hands came loose, and she clawed my back. I was caught off guard. I sat on top of her trying to secure her hand, right then one of her feet came loose and she kicked me in the nuts. This ordeal of hers gave her enough time to untie herself and start running. You know, I don't like hurting women, especially someone like her. She ran violently her bouncing butts were teasing me. Drops of sweat made her dusky body absolutely irresistible. I tackled her down as she was about to leave the room. She fell to the floor, the whole action was so violent that I did not realise that she was not moving until I had entered her from behind and experienced heaven for the next five minutes. It was only then that I saw the pool of blood her head lay in.

I did not expect this. I tried waking her up, but she didn't. That's when I realised that she was gone. I quickly called you to take care of the body and had to take care of the mess before Mukta came home.' I again stopped to listen to what the guy on the other side had to say. But I was barely breathing, I collapsed on the floor near the basin, and my heart was barely beating. The thing with such places is that no one is in their senses to overhear what someone is talking about and why someone is on the floor of a bathroom. I could feel my legs and hands go limp, so I sat on the floor.

He further continued, 'I know it was not the first time it had happened to me. But those girls were already dead to their families and society, so no one ever came looking for them. This one! This one was an extra premium, so the risk was even higher. And the major thing was that Mukta had invited her. I made an excuse to come home early to welcome Pratigya, and to my surprise, she came on time. Poor her, she didn't know that any house party starts an hour late.' Both of them laughed to fill their hearts. I heard him getting up from the pot and making sure that the other person who had done the job would meet him the next day for the payment.

Before he could walk out of the cubicle, I dashed out of the bathroom. HE HAD KILLED PRATIGYA! There was no doubt in my head about what I had to do next. There was nothing left for me to lose, so I went all in. As he came back, he sat where the couple was already waiting for him. I walked to them with drinks. I had already spiked his, and people who are blinded by their lust and confidence will never doubt someone like me. Within a few minutes, he fell unconscious; I offered to handle him as the other two were already sloshed enough to be parcelled back home.

I was the only one sober, so the pub authorities let me take him. I brought him home. He was lying in front of me, completely helpless, just like she would have, when he pounced on her. I had never felt such rage ever before. But I controlled as I didn't want to do anything to him that he could not feel or respond to, or in the worst case, do not remember. I started by stripping him naked and tying him to a chair, with his hand behind the backrest, his feet to the metal base of the chair that had wheels, and his head to the headrest.

I pushed him under the shower and let him get wet with that cold water. I made him sit there till he was alert enough to realise what was happening to him. I then jumped him and pulled his face back, covered it with a towel, and started pouring a mug of water one after another. He was trying to break free from the restraints and shake off the towel as he was struggling to gasp one pinch of air. This is what Pratigya would have felt when that monster was violating her. Then I brought my kitchen scissors, the ones we used to cut chillies, and cut off his eyelids, as he saw me doing that. The pain and the burning made him scream.

Thanks to our soundproof bedroom, our privacy was not intruded upon. He started jumping on the chair, which made the chair move and jump. In his frenzy, one such push made him topple from the chair, and he hit his head on the basin. He didn't move for a few seconds. I thought he was dead. I panicked. I didn't want him to get away this easily. I quickly untied him and rolled him over, to find his lugs still sucking in oxygen. Then I lay him face down with his face hanging off the bed, and tied his hands and legs behind his back together, making him a human bow.

I started a fire under his face and threw a handful of dried red chillies in it. I cut off his eyelids so that it hurt him even when he was unconscious, and waited for him to come back to his senses. He started coughing and sputtering. I sat on him so that he could not move or roll-off, escaping from his agony. He was gasping for breath. I haven't smoked in my entire life, but quenched six cigarettes on his naked and bouncy buttocks and the hole between them. This made him scream, so he had to inhale more air, air filled with smoke from burning chillies. He screamed in pain, which was muffled by the gag.

I enjoyed his helplessness just like he did of my Pratigya. When I felt this was not enough I took the ambers of burnt chillies and shoved it in his ass. When he clenched his hole, I took a bat and pushed it as far as I could. I recalled that I wanted to see the teeth that he used to bite her, so I turned him around, clipped his mouth open and started taking one tooth at a time using a box cutter and a pair of pliers. It was just thirty two times before he gave in and passed out. I waited for him to wake up. Now was the time for the pink patches on his chest! Oh, that was the quickest part. I pulled them till they ripped clean off using the same pliers. Blood ran from his chest to his tool. He was shivering and shuddering in pain. He was bearing this for two days, so he passed out again.

And as Mukta was out of town, our association was uninterrupted. That's when I thought he must be hungry. Since Pratigya had left home, I have not ventured into the kitchen. So the only thing I had was him. I served him with 'his' eggs and sausage when he came out of his cosy slumber. Then I thought of giving him a pedicure. His nails had scratched Pratigya's body and were still dirty. Any other way would not have had an effect on them, so I opened all the nails using a screwdriver. He was shivering with ecstasy!

Lastly, I had to wash her off, his dirty sight. So I took a spoon and scooped his right eye. It popped right off the socket like a ball tied to a cable. He enjoyed the sight with his left eye. But his fun was short-lived. I pulled out his second eye, too. He was about to say something but was busy relishing the taste of his own blood. Now for the main course! He was served with his own excretions, which he could not eat as he passed out as a result of trauma. But don't know why he threw up, cause a man who could enjoy sexual pleasures with a corpse, should enjoy this too.

I thought he wanted me to insist, so I did. I pushed it right down his throat with my own hands. It was not until then that I saw him lying in a pool of blood. And also, he was not moving. That Dr. Raman is my confession." There was silence all around. The faces of all who were listening were white, and their mouths were gaping. With details of what happened to the three lives. The jailer was as stunned as Raman, but he got what he wanted, a proper confession, in grave detail. Raman was still stunned when Sarvadaman said, "I promise I will not turn hostile, but please make sure that I shall not walk free!"

CHAPTER TWO

MOMIYAIWALA

"A beam of bright early morning sunlight slapped my face when my maid withdrew the curtains on my living room window. Well, such a gentle touch can feel like a slap when the last thing you remember was opening the first bottle of whiskey at 9 PM, and then you wake up with a feeling as if your head is being pounded in a rice mortar. Ears ringing, as if my head were inside the bell atop the belfry. Anything below my neck was just lifeless stumps of overgrown flesh, bone, and tissue, which were not expecting any command from my brain. But my brain was receiving constant impulses of pain from it.

My belly was on fire as if someone had poured acid down my throat. Then a jab of realisation hit me; it was none other than me who had done it to myself. Trying to subdue the guilt of being unable to save the person who avenged his beloved. He did exactly what he said to me, "I SHALL NOT WALK FREE"; his words left a scar on my conscience, which I had tried to wipe off by submerging myself in this poison. But to no avail.

Perhaps that was not the only reason for my agony. The constant nagging of this parasite, whom I have hired to take care of my home and make me a meal, which I do not remember. When was the last time I had it? Her complaint brought to my attention that it was not just one bottle of whiskey. It was a pint of rum, three beers, one vodka, and further, going by the ashes, at least two boxes of cigarettes, and a plate of half-eaten chaser was lying all over the floor and, dried retch all over my right foot, my t-shirt, and one side of my face. It was a new low for me, too. I swiftly tried to make my way to the bathroom. It felt like a completely new place for me. I don't know when was the last time I had a proper shower.

My maid was more vocal than usual. She hadn't been quiet since her entry today. It was not what she was saying that bothered me. I wasn't listening to her anyway. Her tone pierced my eardrums like pushing a needle through them. I could not bear it anymore. "AYE! What is it? Don't you understand, how to work without opening your God damn mouth!"

This one act of mine made a lasting impact. There was relief from all the pounding from her deafening voice. The burden of not being able to save an innocent was taking its toll. I mean, he did commit a murder and also confessed to it in front of the judge. There was not much I could've done. But all these are just excuses to clear my conscience so I can look at myself in the mirror. I kept looking at the mirror kept in one side of the room. I did not realise how long I was sitting like that. All I knew was that the sun was setting again. I don't have a clear conscience yet again.

I agree, I have not been myself in a long while. But this version of myself was getting unbearable even for me. So I did the most unlikely thing. "Hello, Sir. I think I need to talk." After a short pause, "Tomorrow, 9 AM, Joggers Park," the voice on the other side of the phone said. The next morning, I was sitting on a bench in the park, looking at the flock of people running past me, leaving me behind. Just like life. Suddenly, I felt the bench was overcrowded. There was a man with a thick white beard, a black tracksuit, and black shades on his eyes. I have never seen his eyes. And I doubt if anyone else has. "Eyes are a reflection of one's mind. And I don't want anyone to know what is going on in here," he said as if he knew what was on my mind.

"What happened to you? You look like a tramp. Not to mention, you smell like a walking liquor store." I was at a loss for words to answer his question. He never looked at me when he talked, yet he was always aware of what I was about to say. He continued, "Sarvadaman was not your mistake. He chose that for himself. And, anyway, you saw what he did to Bhavesh. Just think of it like, there is one less maniac on the streets for us to take care of." I felt violated. "He did not do anything wrong, Captain."

Yes, that's what he was called. No idea why. "He didn't, by killing him. But he did by not hiding it. And as you know, a criminal is one who gets caught." He continued without listening to me, "Have you ever considered seeking help from a professional?" This was the first time I felt violated twice in such a short span. "Help! From a professional! I am a professional…" A large group of senior citizens, above sixty, distracted me as they ran past us, laughing at the top of their lungs. I turned back to Captain to continue my argument in answer to the casual insult he threw at me, but all I found was… A vacant bench, with a packet, where he once sat.

A beam of light from the street lamp fell on a half-empty bottle of whiskey kept in front of me, beside which lay the brown packet. Am I a professional? I mean, I know I was once to whom people came for help, with whom Aditi fell in love, who had all, and then most of her. Later, some, and now none of her. "Ha! Ha! Ha!" A sharp clap and a laugh took me by surprise. "You wish, buddy! You wish! Aditi was just collateral damage for you. You never heard what she had to say, because you were soaring so high. A Protégé! Every news platform, every social media platform, every reporter hunting or pursuing a crime beat, wanted a few minutes of your schedule. Every high-profile case in the country calls for your profiling expertise. But still, you could not save her.

You know why you did not find anything? It's because you did not believe her. Just like everyone else, you too thought she was delusional! Dr. RAMAN SHARMA! YOU… KILLED ADITI! And there is no way you can evade this fact. No matter how much you drown yourself in self-pity and this poison." A man standing in front of me on the other side of the mirror accused me. "HOW DO YOU EVEN DARE TO SPEAK TO ME IN THIS TONE OF VOICE! I loved her! I did everything to save her…" He interrupted me, "Oh Please…. SHUT UP! It was this, your self-righteous platter on which you served her to that monster. It was you who killed her, not him. I was there, I saw you enjoying every moment of her agony." I could not bear it anymore. I picked up the bottle of whiskey and hurled it towards the acid-spitting snake. "I did everything to save her! I turned the world upside down and left no stone unturned to save her. But she just slipped off like sand. I was dying, seeing her going beyond the point of no return. A part of me died that day with her."

The mirror shattered. And so did I. The snake was quiet. In this moment of despair, my mind reminded me of my little rendezvous in the park. I pulled the packet from the table. There was a pager, a few newspaper cuttings, and a note that said, "I take care of men who are useful. Just switch it on when in need." I moved the newspaper clipping under a lamp.

There were multiple news articles presumably about the same case. It was about the disappearance of some local children around a particular locality in Dehradun. All the children were found dead in an abandoned hospital, hanging upside down with pipes protruding out from the back of their skulls. All the male victims had their sexual organs obliterated. And all the female victims were sexually assaulted. All belonged to the eight to twelve years of age group.

The information in my hand resulted from my conscience's desperate cry for help, so before I fell back into the pit of self-realising agony, I knew what to do. I wasted no time in packing my stuff and left for Dehradun. It has been a long while since I last visited this town. My initial days as a consulting clinical psychologist with the local force were here. It is where I was groomed to become who I was before I lost Aditi. I was apprenticing under… (doorbell rings).

The door opened, "Dr. Peter Rebellow?" an aged man in his mid-sixties. A pair of rimless spectacles sat on his nose. His hair was properly combed and held back using gel. With a dark maroon sweater and a pipe in his hand. A pair of dark brown trousers and a pair of leather shoes. The fine wrinkles on his face not only told a tale of a life well-lived, but also a fulfilling one. The stillness in his stance and posture screamed of the strength he possessed in his seemingly old and fragile frame. He responded, "Yes. And who would you… Raman? Is that you?" I smiled and affirmed his statement. "Ha ha ha! What a pleasant surprise. Come here, my boy, let me have a look at you." He held me by my shoulders, shook me heartily, and then held my face, "Ahhh! My protégé." He hugged me tightly, almost filling my void for a companion with a father's touch. My eyes filled up.

I was overwhelmed. "Come, have a seat. Would you like to have tea? Have you had any breakfast? You look thin. Let me fix you with something," he dashed into the kitchen. I stood there, staring outside the window at the lush green hillsides and smoke rising from the chimneys of country houses. Life is slow here, yet refreshing and surprisingly fulfilling. This is what I was missing—the feel of soothing and calm. The cool that quenches one's parched soul. "There you go, my lad. I must say sunny-side-up omelette, with a twist, a Rebellow's special. And the best tea you can find in the area." This was the nicest and freshest meal I had in many years. There was a flood of saliva. It was an explosion of flavours—a symphony in my mouth.

"So what brings you here? And where have you been all this time? And how is Aditi? I want to know everything. Oh God! It has been twenty years since my eyes caught your sight. So go on now, tell me! Tell me everything. I am not used to people talking to me, except my maid. Who does nothing but complain."

"Dr. Aditi is not with us. She died five years ago." The warmth of the living room slowly started to fade away. And was replaced by the chill of melancholy. This was my touch of death.

"I don't know what to say, boy. I mean, how, when! She was so full of life and vibrant. May her soul rest in peace." After a short pause, he continued, "So what brings you here? Vacation?" I answered, slurping tea from the cup, "No, actually…work. Disappearances of local children have caught the eye of a few men in Delhi. They wanted me to rule out any possibility of a serial killer or psychopath at play." He smirked, "So! The devil's back in hell! Ok, I have some contacts in the local police force from my days. Let's see what we can find. I was even wondering about these disappearances. But this does not interest me anymore, so I didn't pursue it further. Let me get ready," he said. I shook my head in affirmation.

"Hello, Inspector Dimri. This is Dr. Raman. He is here to help." He introduced me to the SHO, who welcomed us and gestured for us to sit. "Hello, Sir. I am here to help with the case of those missing children. I need to know when and how this started, and what the findings are so far. I will be helping you to rule out any possibility of a serial killer or psychopath at hand."

"A Serial killer! A Psychopath!" he laughed. And the others laughed with him, "Sir, forgive me, but this is not Delhi. It's a small town. Serial killers and psychopaths don't occur here. No one is greedy in the hills, as the hills have ways to safeguard itself and its people. These disappearances are the work of an organ trafficking cartel, which is part of a bigger drug cartel circulating illegal substances, you know what I mean. You are from Delhi." He said, verbally pointing out my atrocious state of appearance. "Investigation is on. We will nab the culprit or culprits. We don't need your help," he seemed resolute. "Sir, I am on official business." I handed over the letter to him.

Dimri asked me, "Have you been here before, or is this your first time?"

"No, I used to live here. However, this is my first visit in twenty years." I replied.

"Ten years! A lot has changed in ten years. It's almost a new place now. It's a nice place. The weather is great. Have tea, your friend here is a local. Why don't you take him out?" he said, addressing Dr. Rebellow, and then continued, "Come back when you are done enjoying the scenery, we will give you an official report. You take it back. Everyone will be happy."

Dr. Rebellow intervened, "Sir, can we look at the autopsy reports at least? I mean, even he should have something to justify his visit. And I will take him to Joey's tonight," and winked at him.

Inspector Dimri relented and shared the autopsy reports with us. We spent the next few days trying to convince the police to let us help but to no avail.

"This is not the work of any drug cartel or an organ harvesting cartel. All the genitals are 'obliterated', not surgically removed, and all their heads are burnt, like literally charred. This is not a cartel. But the work of a single man, going by the homogeneity. Look at the crude and irregular incisions. The cartel would have sedated the victims to avoid resistance. But the use of ropes and the marks they made clearly suggest that there was a lot of struggle. If it were a cartel, there would be finesse in their work. This is clearly a single man. With no regard for finesse, as if he intended to make the slurry of the organs. And even more, no major organ is missing. Sexual organs! Of children! It's clearly not an organ trafficking cartel. Perhaps, a psycho then!" Dr. Rebellow interjected.

"Ok, if that is the case, then why would he do this? I mean, if we could make a theory, we could pitch our case to SHO Dimri. Then he might even help us find the root cause, and stop these terrible, fateful accidents." I asked him, "Why don't we go and interrogate families and parents of poor children? We will also visit the crime scene. We might find something useful."

Dr. Rebellow affirmed and said, "We'll have to wait till morning. It's almost sundown. People are not welcoming after dark, and it's highly unadvised in the sight of these accidents." I was not a local, and going by the encounter with SHO Dimri, Dr. Rebellow's statement made sense. I held my horses. But could not contain my anticipation. I was bursting with thoughts.

"Let's brainstorm!" I shouted. "Why not? Where should we start?" asked Dr. Rebellow. I quickly turned towards the newspaper clippings, "Here. You see, the way these pipes are inserted. It seems as if there was an attempt to drain something. But it's a very odd position to drain blood from. I mean, if blood is what he wanted, he could have gone for their jugular. Why from behind their heads?" Dr. Rebellow presented a question: "If not blood, then what?"

"There is nothing there but cerebrospinal fluid. But why would someone want CSF? And if that was their target, then why obliterate the sexual organs or assault? And still, the roasting angel is beyond comprehension."

We spent the next few hours trying to put the pieces together, but could not thread all the known facts with one theory. If organ trafficking made sense, then why roast? If torture was the goal, then why drain CSF? And if they wanted CSF, God knows why, why the assault? And most importantly, why only children?

My mind would have imploded in the black hole of these thoughts. "Here, have this. It might help." Dr. Rebellow offered me a glass of single malt. My throat went dry, and my pupils dilated. I literally got an erection. I took the glass with trembling hands. I washed it down my throat, in one gulp. My ears started turning hot. My eyes were watery. It felt like ambrosia. I excused myself and went to the bathroom to relieve myself of this erection. Presumably, I was gone for a little longer than expected, as when I was coming downstairs, I saw Dr. Rebellow, trying to check on me right outside the bathroom door, downstairs. I replied, "Sorry, the bathroom was stinking, I think it's a clogged toilet. I would have thrown up if I had inhaled that stink for even one more second. So I used the one upstairs. I hope it's okay?"

"Absolutely, my lad," he replied joyfully.

"You know, Dr. Raman, these woods are filled with wonders from Mother Earth. Literally gems! But humans are thankless and ignorant imbeciles. We keep working effortlessly, tirelessly, and timelessly to invent and discover new things for ourselves. For our selfish selves. But I am not one of them. I realised my mistake early on. That's when I started venturing into the woods, to understand nature, to seek help and knowledge, and most importantly, to apologise for the deeds of my fellow members of the species. And I must tell you, these woods have taught me what seven years of academics could not.

Every month, I found new plants, new herbs, and shrubs. Fruits, roots, barks, leaves, seeds. I spent years experimenting on them. Creating concoctions, sauces, wafers, and ales. Something like, you just washed down." He walked towards me. Crouched down, held my trousers, and started pulling them. I slid from the sofa, and the glass fell out of my hand; my head banged on the floor. I could feel wet behind my head. But helpless, I was helpless, before blacking out.

I woke up with blurred vision in a dimly lit room. I was seated, resting in a corner of a room which felt like a basement, going by the dampness on its walls. There was a kid hanging upside down in front of me, unconscious, with a cylindrical barrel under her. "You know, what am I going to do here? I am sure you do by now, after all, I trained you. "Why, Dr. Rebellow, why?" I enquired.

He continued, "While I experimented on the flora of these woods, I also extensively travelled throughout the country in search of knowledge. On one such trip to West Bengal, I came across a legend of MOMIYAIWALA SAAB! During the days gone by, it was highly advised that children return home before dark. The whole community was dreaded by the sudden and unexplained disappearances, or rather, unexplained deaths of children. And at the core of this fear was the legend of Momiyaiwala Saab!

There was a belief that a few British officers were so disgusted by their defeat at the hands of such a primitive society that they turned to dark powers in search of ways to reclaim what they believed should never have slipped away. All they needed was time! So through their search, they developed a method that would give them long-lasting life. It was by consuming momiyai.

To test their theory, they would venture into colonies at odd hours and start hunting children to extract their brain matter. Such was their belief: if a child was young, then the extracted brain matter, if mixed with the mush of their sex organs and cooked together, would not only give you eternal life but enhanced human abilities. Isn't it fascinating!" He told me what he did to all those children and what he was about to do to this poor girl. I needed something to stall his actions and came up with a plan."

"That indeed is fascinating. But how did you know that I know about what you have been up to?" I asked him. Dr. Rebellow replied, "I smelled the distinct, peculiar stench of this place on you. I realised that you were on the right track. But what I don't understand is what you found here, because I took all the necessary precautions to hide my tracks?"

He sat right in front of me, staring deep into my soul. I replied, "I did not suspect you until that one night when I had to use the bathroom. It was reeking with the smell of rot. There was dirt and muck on the bathroom floor, which led to the bathtub behind the curtain. When I pushed it aside, I found this little girl unconscious and restrained, lying there. I thought of confronting you, but as I came out, I saw your maid begging for your help to find her daughter, to which you oddly, very coldly replied that you would. That was the only time you let your guard down since I came here, thinking I was not around.

You seemed confident. As if you knew where she was. I saw the stillness in your body language, the calm and soothe in your voice—your trump card. After they were gone, you came to check on her, so I quickly moved upstairs and pretended that I had used the bathroom upstairs, as this bathroom was stinking, because of a clogged toilet. I could see your pupils dilating, your lips drying up, and quickly shifting your weight between your legs. You were barely blinking your eyes.

Everything just became as clear as day. All I wanted was hard proof to back my theory. It was lying in the bathroom." He seemed offended. "HA! HA! HA! HA! So you saw her, huh? Yeah, I had to admit. I was sloppy this one time. I could have done better. But the sheer excitement of playing hide and seek with you forced me to do this," he said, looking at the poor kid.

He turned sharply back to me and continued, "Did I tell you about a tribal ritual from Papua New Guinea? So, the huntsmen of the tribe share the best pieces with all. They eat the part of the animal they hunt, believing that they get the ability of that part of the animal. Isn't it fascinating! I mean, I have heard such claims from many, but this felt scientific! I spent days in the darkest corners of the state, got mugged, and got beaten to the brink of death. But never gave up.

I perfected the recipe of momiyai! It is when the brain matter is cooked in the skull, with the brain flooding with feel-good hormones, which I will share with you. First to find a suitable subject, today we have Priyanka, who is the daughter of my maid. "Priyanka! Say hi to Dr. Uncle's friend." He took her hand, which was tied behind her back, and continued. "She is very bright. Top of her class. Wants to be an IAS officer. Hence, it will help us tonight with this demonstration. We first start…" She was gagged. She looked at me with hope. But I was unable to move myself. I desperately tried to help her, "It's very unlikely of you, Doc." He stopped sharply and turned towards me, "I mean. You were never this clumsy and disoriented. You always planned your actions and made sure you enjoyed the process. So why the hurry? Are you scared?"

He was triggered. As he walked back to me, I could feel that he was losing his grip. I was in control now! "Ok, so let me explain the perfect recipe for momiyai. We begin by starting a fire under her and increasing it till the flames start reaching her head. Gradually, her hair will catch fire. It is the exact moment when we douse the fire on her head and bring her down. This is done to increase the feel-good hormone in her brain.

Then I strip her naked and massage her head and body. Then enter her. It is also necessary for us to feel good, hence I make sure to enjoy the process. I keep pounding her with all my might till I am done. Her body is so sleek and tender. I must taste it. It's good for the skin. A piece of her chest, modesty, and hips will do just fine. Then, I'll put her on the rope again and start the fire. She will be shivering with pain. Her flesh will start melting and dripping in fire. We have to repeat this process till she stops moving naturally. Then I'll bring her down again and help my way in her. She is a bit tight, you know, so it's an effort, but the second time she will be fully lubricated and wet. You see, I told you she has to feel good.

Then, eventually, she will stop fighting for her life. Now, this is the most important part, as it took me years to reach this point. We crack open a hole in the back of her head, push a silicone pipe and suck on the other end of it. A viscous liquid will start to flow out and fall into a bowl kept below. You know Raman, the best momiyai is made when the brain matter is cooked slowly with the brain high on endorphins and used as a wok in the skull. I will let you taste it. Once the flow stops, Dr. Rebellow will pick it up and, without taking a breath, slurp it whole."

I was stunned by the grave detail in which he had tortured those kids before her. I could see his eyes glimmering with pride and satisfaction, but mainly because he had defeated me, as I would not be able to help her, but die. I had to go all in. "Ooofff! You've had a pretty busy last few years! But well-spent ones. However, doc, you explained how, but my question was, why?"

He replied, "I will clear this doubt for you. I was the best in my world. Leagues ahead of any other. I drew the attention of national media to this otherwise unknown town. I was the front page bit of every new paper in the country. People literally feared me. Till… till you came here. I shared everything I knew. Every damn trick of the trade. And you learnt them well, and you learnt them quickly. So, obviously, I had kept all the tricks up my sleeve. But you, you learnt them on your own. Things that I took years to learn and even longer to master, came to you naturally. Everything I tried to hide from you, you excelled at it in a short time. You were a natural. And you surpassed me.

Eventually, I became a faded star under your lustre. A forgotten name. No one came to me; everyone wanted you. My stature was reduced to a mere assistant. You replaced me on all the newspapers and channels. You were my Able! YOU SNATCHED EVERYTHING FROM ME! EVERYTHING THAT I WORKED FOR. MY EMPIRE I BUILT BRICK BY BRICK. And you! You hijacked my stardom. So now, I will have my share of recognition. Remember I told you how the Guinean tribesmen eat a specific part of their hunt, to enhance that ability in themselves? I have had enough momiyai, I can have it later, as much as I want. But today, I will have you!

You know, Raman, I have never had anyone's brain before. But you, it's your brain! That is what makes you special. Now I will have it." He picked me up by my shoulders and made me sit in a chair. Then he pulled the drawer of the table kept at the end of the room, and walked back with a scalpel. As he started cutting through my skin, I realised I could feel it now. It was at this moment that I closed my eyes, and all I could remember was the time I spent with Aditi. I saw her! She held me by my hand and said, "It's okay, let it go. It's not your fault."

Suddenly, there was a loud bang, and the door of the basement fell open. Six policemen rushed in. The bang caused the scalpel to fall out of Dr. Rebellow's hands. I quickly pushed myself away from him and fell on the floor. There was a loud blast, and I passed out due to the impact. The next few visuals were flashy. I was being carried out, the girl was with her mother, Dr. Rebellow's body was being packed in a body bag, I was put in an ambulance, and the doors were shut. My eyes opened in the hospital. I saw a nurse standing by my side and adjusting my cannula. "I will call the officers in," she said, walking right out the door. I could see Satya and Vrinda next to me.

SHO Dimri walked in and explained that they got an anonymous call and a location to reach the church. He handed me a pager with "Gottcha! Kid" displayed on it.

The pager I had received in the packet with newspaper clippings of the case came in handy. When I regained my senses in the corner of the church's basement, I knew I could not handle this alone. Surprisingly, I switched on the pager that I had on me. It was not a pager but a homing beacon under the shell. Dr. Rebellow would not have thought that such a primitive piece of tech would get him caught.

CHAPTER THREE

RAKTABEEJ

"My vision, for the next few weeks, was nothing but flashes of different people looming over me, police officers checking on me for my statement, a nurse cleaning and wiping me and changing my drip, and Satyabhama and Vrinda visiting me multiple times.

"There was an asura king called Danu. His two sons, Rambha and Karambha, who had no children, did *tapas* at *panchanda* for the blessing of having children. Rambha and Karambha meditated upon the gods for aeons, at the centre of the five fires, and the latter standing in the water of a lake. *Indra* found out about this, he decided to kill them.

First, in the guise of a crocodile, he dragged *Karambha* away by the feet and killed him by drowning him. Then *Indra* went after *Rambha* to kill him, but Agni saved him. Angry at the death of his brother, *Rambha* decided to cut off his head and offer it as a sacrifice. When he was about to do so, *Agni* appeared and told him that suicide was worse than killing others, denouncing it as a great sin, and promised to grant him whatever he desired.

Accordingly, *Rambha* requested Agni for a son more effulgent than the latter, who would conquer the three worlds and would not be defeated by the gods and the demons. *Rambha* further wanted his son to be as powerful as the wind God, Pawan, exceptionally handsome, and skilled in archery.

Agni blessed *Rambha* so that he would have, as desired, a son from the woman he coveted. On his way home, he saw a beautiful she-buffalo, *Mahiṣī*, which he married. He took the buffalo to the netherworld, the *Patala*, to protect it from being attacked by other buffalo.

One day, another buffalo felt a passion for Rambha's wife, and in the fight, Rambha was impaled with the buffalo's horns, killing him. Later, the water buffalo was killed by Rambha's soldiers. Rambha's wife died in his funeral pyre after jumping into it. It was from the centre of the fire that the very powerful *Mahishasura* was born. Rambha also rose from the fire under the name *Raktabīja* along with his brother, *Mahishasura*. *Raktabīja* secured a boon from Lord Shiva, according to which if one drop of blood from his body fell on the battlefield, many Raktabījas would arise from the blood and fight the enemies. Each of these Raktabījas would also be like the others in the matters of strength, form, and weapons."

"Really, Mummy! With every drop, one more demon. Then it will be impossible to kill him, won't it? Then how will they kill him?" I heard Vrinda asking an innocent question to Satyabhama, my sister, and the only known relative I relate to. She replied, "You know, Vrinda, that our scriptures are beautifully written in prose to capture the essence and impart more than eyes could see and read. So, Rakhtabeej could also be understood as the ill intentions and foul practices prevalent in our society and done by a few bad people."

Satyabhama stopped as she saw me, coming out of my coma. She quickly ran towards me, then out of the room. I saw a doctor and nurses running into the room, and Satyabhama behind them. I again saw their worried faces as they tried to get a response from me. But their voices seem like coming from the other end of the tunnel.

I don't know how long I was out after this episode. But then, suddenly, I saw Aditi sitting on a chair on the balcony of our bedroom. Her hair was damp, and a steaming cup of coffee was clasped between her palms. She had a white translucent shirt that loosely fit her. I slowly got up from my bed and started walking towards her. Surprisingly, it was not too much of an effort. She hummed our song, *"Zindagi ko pyaar bina koi kaise guzare…"*

She was unaware of my existence in the scene. I could see her through the shirt. Droplets trickling down her back and reaching the dimples at the bottom of her spine were like a flood in the parched desert land. Folds on her skin, on the sides of her back, felt like layers of butter, sliding against each other from a stack. As she brought the cup close to her lips to take a sip of coffee, her hair slid to one side, exposing her neck.

As the shirt collar was lying low, I could see well below her shoulders. Tiny water droplets on her neck sat as pearls without a thread, each illuminated like a sun. Her golden chain, which ran around her neck, seemed like a thread of saffron on the surface of milk. She was radiating light and smelled of sandalwood treated with coffee. A ray of sun fell on her ear as she tucked her hair behind it. As she turned a bit, a glare from the tip of her nose stung my eyes. I fell to my knees, as I realised how long it had been since I saw her. It was this sound that made her aware of my puny existence, as she got up and quickly turned to fill my face in her palms, "Aye, what happened. Take it easy. It's okay. I am here." I could not open my eyes to look at her to the fullest. Suddenly, I saw two nurses rushing in, holding me by my arms, trying to pick me up from where Satyabhama sat, holding my face.

Everything felt so heavy and slow, and my inability to do something about it added to my frustration. I gave up on my will to live. I felt a heavy pounding on my chest, and the frantic attempts of panicking faces of the hospital staff made it clear that my wish had been granted. I again faded into slumber. I woke up to my full senses, I don't know how much time. But it was well over a month and a half, most of which I could not attempt to remember, but was well documented with overgrown hair and facial hair that I saw in a mirror on the wall on my left side. It was an early hour of the day. I could hear the beeping of machines around me. I saw Satyabhama and Vrinda curled up against each other on a couch.

I called out, "Satya!" She woke up suddenly and, seeing me in her full senses and alive, ran towards me. She hugged me tightly, almost smothering me, disregarding the fact that I was literally dead a while back. She looked at me with tears in her eyes. She has been my mother since our parents passed away. Once she made sure I were not a dream, she called for the doctor and the next hour went by in medical examination.

"You are lucky, Mr. Raman, to have survived. Though it might not look much on the outside, on the inside it was a total mess. And not only that, somewhere along the way, it felt like you didn't want to get through this. Anything that I must know? Anything that police might find? Anything that might make you end up here, cause you know, Dr. Raman, this is a small town, and it's not ready for what comes with you. So, please, next time, choose a different city. But for now, take rest and we will keep monitoring you."

I asked desperately, "How long could it be?" The doctor replied, "Could be a week or a month. Don't worry, you will know." And walked out of the room. Satyabhama walked up to me, "So, finally, I get to talk to my little brother," she said, to which I replied with a nod. "Don't you think it's time for you to take a break? You have been torturing yourself for a long while. I am worried about you. This way you will stay close and our little Vrinda here will also enjoy the company of her favourite uncle." She lifted Vrinda and kept her on her lap. "How are you, Mama?" she asked.

"I am fine. I see nothing has happened to me. I just had not slept in many days, and I also don't like going to the office like you don't like going to school, so I played a prank on the doctor and your mumma, that I have a severe stomach ache. So they let me sleep." Another one of her innocent questions came, "Where did it hurt? Here?" she pointed towards her belly. "There and, there and there…"

I started tickling and poking her, to which she broke up hilariously. Her contagious laughter caught hold of me and my sister. Then we shared everything that happened over the span of time since we last saw each other. "Ha… ha…ha…ha…, really? Oh my God! I can't believe it. Oooff! I can even remember how much I have missed laughing like this. I don't remember when I last laughed like this." I said. "So why don't you come and live with us?"

"Yes, Mama, come live with us, please," said Satya and Vrinda. A nurse entered the room and asked them to let me rest. Vrinda was adamant about staying the night. Satya somehow managed to convince her to leave. I didn't want them to leave, but I needed rest. It was quiet since they left. The constant beeping of the machines was the only relief from this deafening silence. Suddenly, my pager, which was kept on the side table, beeped. "Welcome back, kid." I was surprised. How did he know that I was out of the coma? The very next message said, "I take care of people who are useful." This cleared my doubt. I thought of going back to sleep, a brief one.

The next morning was closer to what one could consider normal. It wasn't much after nine, and after the nurse had served me my breakfast, Satya and Vrinda came to visit me. She ran and jumped into my arms. I had missed her so much. "She had made it impossible for me to focus on anything from last night. 'When will we go to visit him? When will we go to visit him? When will we go to visit him? When will we go to visit him?' Agh! So here is your uncle; and, Uncle, here is your niece…" Before she could say anything. I waved for her to come and join the hug. She jumped with joy and hugged us tightly. We stood there for a while. "See, I have a very important meeting for which I have to travel back to Delhi. I cannot take her with me. So could you please keep an eye on her?" I nodded back, affirming. Then she turned to Vrinda, "I have packed your lunch, snacks, and activity books in this bag. I will be back by dinner. So don't trouble your uncle. He is still recovering." Vrinda nodded adorably. "Ok then, all set. Take care, both of you. See you soon," Satya waved and left.

Vrinda and I sat there talking about all sorts of stuff. Right from her classroom gossip to her playground excellence. How Vishakha from her class always gets her in trouble, but because Vrinda is such a good girl, and their teacher knows it, she always comes to rescue her whenever the matter escalates to their principal. "I already like your principal, she seems smart," I said.

"She is old, Mama. Her kids are almost your age. And anyway, she is not your type." She dismissed my interest in her principal. My eyes widened. How much she had grown. "What happened to Maami?" She asked hesitantly. I was dumbstruck, not knowing what to say. "Mmm… I will tell you everything after lunch." I took a narrow escape. For the next hour, I tried everything to take her mind off her question. We called Satya and talked about how our day was going, how her day went, and how bland the hospital food was.

I wanted a part of Vrinda's lunch. But she turned out to be stricter than Satya. Then asked when she would be back. I assumed that Vrinda would abandon her chain of thought from before the meal, and I would not lapse into the trap of my past and guilt. She lay there beside me, I was reading her a story from the book she picked, and it was right then, "You said you would tell me after lunch. But it's okay if you don't want to. I understand." I actually didn't want to tell her! Firstly, because it's not something a kid is supposed to know. But moreover, I myself didn't want to tread on the trail that I had tried so hard to let the grass grow. "What do you remember of her?" I caved in and asked Vrinda. But only to my relief, she had fallen asleep. But now the chain reaction had initiated.

"I was new in the city of Delhi, and I was called in as a consultant on a case of a very weird sort. It was a case of young, vulnerable men who had fallen prey to substance abuse and were admitted to a rehab centre. They were getting raped and brutally murdered! Yes… Men… Raped… It had stunned the capital like nothing before. So there was a lot of buzz in the media and masses, and many NGOs and non-profits were clawing at the police and authorities. Hence, they wanted me to profile the person on the loose and go berserk on the streets. I ventured into the autopsy reports of the victims, and it turned out that it all started in one corner of the city.

Suddenly, the epicentre shifted to a rehab home on the city's other side. Another peculiar thing was, though they were raped, their male genitalia we surprisingly unharmed and also no damage to the anal tract! What was absurd was that their chests were completely obliterated, with their ribs broken at multiple places, the sternum literally shattered, and the heart and lungs punctured by bone fragments ranging from point one millimetre to two centimetres, providing evidence of multiple blunt force trauma.

Their necks were filled with hickeys, so hard, that multiple victims had a blood clot due to such hard sucking, and that clot travelled to their brain and in some cases to their hearts that caused a stroke and heart attack. Their body was filled with patches of their own semen and fingerprints, showcasing that these were the doings of a man with large hands. Their anal tract also had semen traces of their own which was homogenous across all the victims. This case was really a doing of either someone who really enjoys doing this and considers it their hunt, or he does it out of compulsion, as and when he gives in to his sinister sexual urges.

I decided to visit the rehab where the last two victims were before they were molested. It was there that I saw Aditi for the first time. The air hung thick and humid, a typical summer evening in the city. I was rushing to find out more about the case at Ground Zero. My mind was a jumble of to-do lists, a far cry from romantic thoughts. And then I saw her. She was standing by the corner flower stand, bathed in the warm glow of the setting sun. She wore a simple white dress that flowed around her like a whisper, and her dark hair was pulled back in a loose bun, a few strands escaping to frame her face. I slowed my pace, suddenly finding myself unable to look away. As if sensing my gaze, she turned. Time seemed to stop. Her eyes, a startling shade of coffee, met mine, and a jolt of electricity shot through me. It was a connection so immediate, so visceral, it took my breath away. For a moment, the world around me faded. The noise of the city and the jostling crowd ceased to exist. There was only her, her eyes holding mine in a silent conversation that transcended words. A small, almost hesitant smile played on her lips, and my heart did a somersault. I don't know how long I stood there, locked in that silent exchange. It could have been seconds, it could have been minutes. It felt like an eternity.

Finally, a car horn blared nearby, jolting me back to reality. I blinked, the spell broken. She glanced away, a faint blush rising on her cheeks. She turned back and asked me to follow her inside. She understood that I was with the police because a looming figure was behind me. It was at this time that I realised that Vrinda was fast asleep. But I must continue the tale if I have to tell you everything.

She went and sat in the chair behind a desk. 'Please sit,' She pointed towards the chair. The constable rushed from behind me, swiftly sat on the left chair, and pulled out his hand to introduce himself, "Hello, Madam! Myself, Jaya Prakash Chaurasiya. Head Constable, Delhi Police." She shook his hand, and panned her gaze to me, "And you are?" I was still under her spell, which broke with Chaurasiya's attempt to clear his throat. "I… I am Raman Sharma, a consultant with the Delhi police." She exclaimed, "Oh! A detective! So this case is not worthy of mainstream investigation."

Chaurasiya interjected, "No, no! Madam, it is a very interesting case. That's why we have asked for the help of a clinical psychologist to profile whether there is a serial or psycho killer on our hands." Chaurasiya, gleaming with pride, looked at me with a wide smile, just like a child after a good poem recital, where everyone was clapping for it. "Oh, sorry, I thought you were a consulting detective. Hi, I am Aditi. I run this NGO. We work for underprivileged men, mostly boys, struggling with substance abuse and alcoholism. We re-establish them in society." I was still staring at her. Gaping.

Again, Chaurasiya helped me come back to reality, "Oh! I am sorry. I zoned out. So, when did this start happening? And do you have any reason in mind that this could be happening only to this NGO? I mean, is there anyone you suspect?" I asked her. Chaurasiya pulled out a notepad and started taking notes. "I really am surprised why only this NGO. I have no enemies. We have always worked together with the local administration and the forces. We have not gotten anyone in trouble nor gotten into one ourselves." She answered. "What about property disputes? Who owns this land?" I enquired further.

"I own this land. It's an ancestral property. And we have renovated my father's ancestral home into a dorm," she explained. "How many brothers did your father have?" I pressed further. "My father had an elder brother and a younger sister. But they have got their share of my grandfather's property." I stayed silent. She continued, "All I can say is, it feels like I have made the hunt easier for the wolf by keeping all the sheep together." Something clicked. "Can you give me a record of all the employees, full-time and volunteers, who frequently visit here with their background verification?" I asked. She complied, "Yes, sure, it's all in our record room. But I don't know if this will be of any help, as we go through a thorough background and medical examination before we let anyone in." She called in the peon and asked him to walk us to the record room.

It took us hours to go through all the records, but everything was in place, perfectly spotless, with no sign of any foul play. I started spending time at the NGO to gather more and more information. Establish people's behavioural patterns, visiting patterns, eating habits, and personal preferences. Aditi had shifted her residence to NGO premises to help fast-track the investigation.

During this time, we got close. We started spending time together to discuss the case, scouring traces of evidence and also recreation. And I did not realise when we became more than just friends. The comfort we had with each other was unfelt by us before. It was on one such night that I was walking her to her bungalow. "So!" I asked her. "So!" She replied. "It seems we should call it a night. It was a fruitful day. I learnt a lot of new things," I said.

She shook her head, looking down at the floor, blushing, and tucked her hair behind her ear. I said goodbye and was about to turn when I saw her opening the lock on the door. Then, suddenly, I felt a strong pull on my arm, which made me twist, and her lips landed on my cheek. Everything came to a standstill. I could see her pacing back in her room. I wanted to hold her and kiss her back, taste her lips, smell the sandalwood perfume that she uses off her neck, hold her by her waist, and against the wall, kiss her on her face and on her ear, inhaling the intoxicating fragrance of her hair, then pulling them back, exposing her décolletage. Her smooth skin would be glistering with sweat from anticipation and thrill. Her rapid breathing will emphasise her perfectly proportioned chest, and the hollow between them would smell like roses and coffee. All this made me utterly immovable. It took me some time to realise that her door was kept open.

I cautiously opened the door, thinking with my brain. "You took time to process it," she said, sitting on the chair in front of a dressing table. With wet hair tied up in a high bun, her black gown sat very low on her back, which was covered with tiny droplets of water. I could not resist myself and walked towards her. To my surprise, she got up as I approached her and pushed me onto her bed. I fell on a firm yet soft mattress, with my legs bent from the knee down. She then bent and started taking off my shoes. I helped myself up and saw the real beauty. Her gown revealed enough to make me go crazy, but also just enough to make me intrigued.

She then stood up and pushed me down on the bed once again. She then lifted her gown to knee length. A ray of moonlight in the dimly lit room made her skin look like molten silver and gold blending into each other. Then, with a smooth motion of her hips, she climbed and sat on my thighs. Her fingers started to slide from my thighs to my waist, and then under my shirt, with her perfectly balanced on me. My shirt lifted, exposing my belly button. She had maintained proper eye contact with me this whole time. She looked like an enchantress, and I could do nothing to help or evade the situation.

As she moved further, her bun came loose, and her damp, heavy locks fell on my bare skin, sending goose bumps throughout my body. Then she leaned and kissed my navel, then slightly above it, then slightly below it. I didn't even realise when she undid my belt and slid my trousers and underwear down my legs. There was nothing to hide now. We have long crossed the point of no return. She kept her fingers around it at its base and pulled the skin back.

I could not see anything as the action was veiled by her thick black hair. But that was the exact moment I realised the role of touch among our five senses. The warmth of breath, and the sensation of her wet mouth and her soft lips, as they went up and down on it, made me feel like sinking into bed. I could not be a mere spectator anymore; I had to participate. I placed my hand on her head and tried to lift my waist. But she jerked my hand off. She lifted her head up and flipped her hair back, wiping her lips with the sleeve of her gown.

This was my chance to grab the glory. I too sat upright and started lifting the cloak that had covered her body, made of glass till now. Her modesty was rubbed against it. I then took off my shirt. We were naked! In front of each other. Her skin, though fair, glowed like copper. I turned and pinned her on the same bed, on which I was stapled till now. I traced every millimetre of her body with my lips. His periodic sighs were an indication of her agreement and pleasure with my actions.

Slowly, I kissed her navel, she twisted with a sharp sigh, her eyes clenched, and a light smile on her lips. I traversed up from there and reached her chest, which was firm, sturdy, yet soft. I moved my tongue around her areola. She again flinched. Then, pressed it between my teeth. She cried in pain and slapped me. I had to teach her a lesson. I made my way to its cousin, but his time I placed my arms under her right knee and lifted her waist a little. And before she could realise what was about to happen, I thrust myself into her. And before she could respond to this, I again bit her on her perky melon. All this was too much for her. She embraced me tightly and made me taste her tongue as tears rolled down her eyes. Then the final act of love was done. I kept throbbing inside her, and she kept her allegiance by keeping the ground of action moist.

Those were the early hours of the next morning; she was lying next to me, sleeping peacefully like a newborn child. It was then that I heard fast and heavy footsteps outside our room. I got up and swiftly covered myself to check who it was. To my surprise, it was not a single person, but people.

The house that was quiet at night now seemed like a hostel. There were people cleaning the house, some were taking clothes for laundry, some were having breakfast, and some were cooking. There were some people walking with files and documents with them and talking about something that seemed important. "This bungalow is not only my personal residence but the residence of staff who have nowhere to go. We give them employment and also a place to call home." She explained everything from the bed.

As I was making my way back inside, I saw a lady orderly standing next to me. "I am Anupama. I am a cook. Can you please ask Madam what she would like for breakfast?" I was startled by the authority and command with which she approached me. Big eyes with kohl, a big red *bindi,* a light-coloured saree, a pendant in a gold chain that sits perfectly on her deep-cut neck, a perfectly fitting full-sleeved blouse, broad shoulders, and a proud build, with a sweet voice. "Oh! Anupama. Great that you are here. Please, can you make your famous dhokla for me? I am super hungry." Aditi came out of the room, all dressed and ready for the day. Anupama left, but before she left us, she looked at both of us, blushed, and ran away.

"So, you are ready for the day?" Aditi came close to me and placed her hands on my shoulders. "Who was she?" I asked, un-wavered by the sheer ecstasy in Aditi's eyes. "Who! Anupama?" Aditi replied and continued to elaborate. "She is here as a part of the pantry staff. She has amazing voice modulation talent, she can mimic anyone just by hearing their voice for the first time."

Satisfied, or rather, being uninterested in a voice artist. I interjected, "Yeah! But I want to talk about the night." I tried to grab her and take her inside the room, but before I could do that, she was called for urgent official business. She left me to get ready. I walked into her office after some 45 minutes and saw a huge crowd already present there. I made my way through the crowd and next to Aditi, who was trying to handle them. "What happened, Chaurasiya?" I asked.

"There was one more murder yesternight here." It was a cold blow to my mind, and I was still stuck on what had happened in that room last night. A murder! A cold-blooded murder! Happened right under our noses, and we were making love. Chaurasiya continued, "These staff members found the body behind the bungalow and want to leave the job." Aditi was trying to convince them to stay back, but the union was led by Anupama, who would not relent.

After arguing for hours, some people broke ranks and stayed back. But most followed Anupama and left. The next few days were quite tight. With fewer caregivers, it was difficult to take care of the boys in rehab. Although in the light of these gruesome murders, many of them have also checked themselves out, and some have fled. But we were still responsible for at least the dozen souls, whom she saw as her own brothers.

Aditi was drowning in trying to keep the centre afloat. I could not see her like this, and with the investigation not moving forward and the waters calm, I came up with a plan. "Will you marry me?" I asked her. Sitting on a knee, in her office, with almost all the caregivers and the boys around. I meant it as a surprise to jerk her out of the gloom, but it seemed that beside her, everyone else was happily surprised, but she; she was shocked. The cold trail of the case took everyone's attention off the rehab centre, and it gave us relief and a window to sneak some festivities in. But she did not forget about the ones who had lost their lives here. As a result, the centre would serve as the venue for the big fat event.

Eventually, the night came. The whole centre was draped in flowers, and what was not covered by flowers was covered by lights. All the patients partook in the festivities, arrangements, and ceremonies as Aditi's brothers. They even prepared a dance for her on her favourite song *"Zindagi ko bina pyaar koi, kaise guzaare."* Everything was great, and it even seemed to come back on track. Till that night when I was returning back from a conference, but was running late. When I came back, I saw all the bungalow lights on, which was very unusual for the time. As I went inside, I saw all the caregivers gathered around on the first floor, outside our room.

As I moved through the crowd, I saw sister Avantika sitting on the bed with Aditi's head on her lap and weeping profusely. She saw me and came and clung to me like a joey to its mother, and kept crying for the next hour. All my efforts to console her were in vain. But all I could understand were a few words like 'bhoot', 'bhoot'...... that came out of her mouth. I instantly grew a grin and looked up, only to find everyone else's expression telling me to take this seriously. I tried to console her, "Okay, okay, it's okay. See, I am here, all of us are here for you. And the ghost....it's gone. Just calm down."

It took us a few hours and we retired into our beds for the night, close to dawn. The next morning was rather calm. And so was the next year. But the days after that brought a new chaos after we had moved to my home. With the gruesome fatalities stopped and murders of some poor addicts, who, according to the police, would have died anyway, not glamorous enough, this seemed a logical move. It was a humble abode, a classic Indian house. Two bedrooms, that open into a dining cum living space, a kitchen attached to it and a drawing room separated by translucent curtains. An ally at the back of one of the rooms, with an opening in the ceiling for ventilation, opens up at the rooftop, which housed all my plants, and parking in the front.

I was at home when I heard Aditi coming back in after a shopping spree. "It was so tiring, we did a lot of shopping. We brought a bachelorette dress for Samidha, a birthday gift for Shamal's boyfriend, a few things for ourselves, and… for you, a really cute… *Arey!* Where did it go? I think I left it in the car. I will just bring it!" She showed me everything they had bought, and for the things she did not buy, she showed me the photographs. Suddenly, I heard a loud scream from outside; I ran to check on her. She was hanging out of the driver's seat, hyperventilating, trying to get out of the car, but couldn't as her foot got stuck in this frantic attempt. I ran towards her, trying to pick her up into the driver's seat, but she pushed me away, making me trip as she went a little inside the vehicle. Then she got out and ran into the house.

I was sitting on the road, trying to process everything. I went in, trying to find her, but she was nowhere to be found. She was not responding to my voice. Then, the sound of running water was caught by my auditory receptors. I rushed towards our bathroom and slightly pushed the door, which fell open. I saw Aditi frantically trying to wipe off something. Her agitated movement has left scratches and rashes on her back, neck, face, and around her chest. Where I could now visibly see a palm print, as she was groped. I understood the reason behind her outburst, so I walked towards her and hugged her tightly, to which she retaliated, but upon realising that it was me, she settled into my arms. Crying. We sat there under the shower for hours, crying.

Later that night, while applying ointment on her deep scratches, she told me what had transpired with her. "I went outside to bring in the t-shirt, which was lying in the car's back seat. So I opened the door and grabbed it. Then I saw my charging cord in front. So I closed the back door and sat in the driver's seat to check if there was anything else I was forgetting. Suddenly, what I feel is a tight, firm grip that covers my mouth, suffocating any scream deep in my throat. Then another hand came from the other side and started squeezing me. Squeezing everything that it can get. Then a masked face, covered from head to nose, leaned forward and started kissing and licking me on my neck, back, and face through the mask. Then it spoke in a thin voice, 'You are delicious. Worthy enough to be touched. I love the likes of you, right amount of flesh in the right places. I have always coveted your attention whenever you pass by me. But then you gave yourself to him." He was about to put his other hand in my kurti, and that's when I got a chance to bite his hand. The moment he lost his grip, I screamed. But he got away."

She was crying over what had happened to her, right outside of the house, which she thought was the safest place. And I was crying because I could not make it safe for her. The night went by. She slept next to me with the attention of a dog. Seeing her waking up at every unexplained noise of the night broke my heart. But it was just the start of the never-ending darkness of our lives.

I tried getting help from the police. We patrolled the places that she frequently visited and rounded up everyone who was under suspicion multiple times. A patrol vehicle was stationed at each entry and exit lane of our colony. Cameras were installed on the entry, roof, and two light poles. But we hit a dead end everywhere. As the incident had no witnesses or proof, the police entourage was soon revoked. I was left with no choice but to do it myself. But it was not enough. She was getting teased and groped and touched and assaulted repeatedly, and now with even higher frequency. But one thing was common, NO EYE WITNESSES! So it was nearly impossible to convince the police that it was really happening to us.

Consequently, it gave rise to suspicion of domestic violence by me. So we started avoiding going to the police. My regular AWOLs started taking a toll on my work. Thinking that the surveillance cameras around our house were the only respite, Aditi stopped leaving the house. She was cornered like a predator hunting its prey. Things between us were getting worse with every passing day. She started seeing me as the perpetrator. She started avoiding talking to me, eating at the same table, and sleeping on the same bed, so much so that she even stopped sharing the same room. I could see her condition deteriorating.

It had been six months, so one day, I decided to confront her. "Aditi, can we talk?" I asked her. Instantaneously, I saw her getting alert as a gazelle would get near the river in the morning, once it got the visual of a tiger. "Yeah... Say?" she timidly asked. "What is going on between us? Why are we living as strangers under the same roof? I understand we are going through a difficult situation, but at least, can we not turn our backs on each other? It's getting difficult for me." Her expressions changed in response to my argument. "Difficult for you, Raman? I am the one being treated like a rag doll, whom he can come and play with anytime he wants."

I countered, "I know! I am not denying the fact. I am doing everything I can possibly do, but..." She interrupted me, "But, what but? Great Dr. Raman Sharma profiled so many psychos but was not able to catch his wife's perpetrator. Raman, I am your wife, not another victim. You should have caught him by now. But you are not able to do it because you are not at peace. You know how it feels when I step out of the main gate? How do people see me? The questions in their eyes. Their audacious attempts to see beneath my clothes, to see if I am really worth it. From the milkman to the newspaper hawker, everyone expects answers from me. ME!" I tried to save myself," I get it, but it's not just you who is facing the world, I am, too, facing the world. The same eyes are asking me questions too. Expecting explanations. To which I have no evidence of..." Her crying interrupted me. "You need evidence?" She got up and took off her oversized turtle neck. Her body was filled with bruises and marks. Bruises on her inner thigh and hands. Bite marks on her upper chest and back. It looked like she had been in an animal attack. "Leave!" She dictated.

"I am sorry, Aditi, I didn't know about all this." And took a step towards her. "STOP RIGHT THERE, RAMAN!" she said with a resolution in her voice. I was stunned. "LEAVE NOW," she continued. I was numb and left the room as if I were a spring-powered top that was cranked and kept on the floor. I came out of the house and started walking. Actually, I was trying to evade the voice of her mournful cry, as it was piercing my façade of fake manhood and exposing my impotency.

I started walking faster until I felt her voice fading, and I kept walking. I was talking to myself, "I mean, I was trying everything I could. I tried reaching out to the police, I've tried following her myself, rounded up all the suspects, and even installed security cameras. What else could I have done? It's not that she is the only one stuck in this, I am also being grounded with her. I understand it's a bit more on her, but..."

A car blew its horn as it passed by, very close to me, and pulled me out of my argument, which I was about to lose. It was then that I realised that I had come very far from home, and it had been hours since I left. Not just my physical home, but hers. And no matter what I do or how hard I try, I cannot understand what she is going through. Her pain is incomprehensible, and my behaviour has only added to her helplessness.

I start running back to my house with eyes wide open and only one thing on my lips, "I AM SORRY, ADITI. I LOVE YOU, AND I SHOULDN'T HAVE LEFT." As I reached my home, I was hit by a strong, cold breeze of isolation. The main gate was ajar. I quickly went in and saw she had not locked the bedroom door. My eyes went wide, and I rapidly went inside, absolutely panting, but what I saw took my breath away. Aditi lay on the bed with her eyes wide open, with tears rolling down from the corner, naked, with blood oozing from the sheets and flowing along the bed into a puddle of blood on the floor. Her mouth was gagged with a piece of cloth. Her chest was open and her insides were exposed as if a speeding truck had hit her head-on. Her hands fell on each side as they were tired of trying to hold onto life just long enough for me to return. Her feet tried their best to take her away from here, but could not as they were broken at the ankle. Her front bottom was swollen and was oozing blood. I could not stand the sight; my vision became hazy, and I collapsed. I was hoping that when I woke up, this all would be revealed as a dream.

But to my horror, I woke up hours later to the sight of that puddle of blood, which was not collecting any more as the blood had gotten thick and flies were hovering over it. I slowly and trembling got on all my fours and helped myself up to see her lifeless body still gazing at the wall, and a conclave of flies all over her. I again fell to my knees and could do nothing but just shout at the top of my lungs. I shouted and shouted and kept shouting till I could not anymore. I cannot even try to explain the pain I felt at that moment, which was unbearable. I felt some neighbours had entered and held me. I was wheezing, as I could not shout any more. My eyes were flooded, and my nose started to bleed. That's all I could remember before I passed out again.

I opened my eyes to Chaurasiya and a few other police officers around me in a hospital. I immediately realised what had happened before and tried to get up, but found myself handcuffed to the bed. "What is this, Chaurasiya? Huh.? Why did they have to handcuff me? Huh?" I asked but lost my cool, "ANSWER ME DAMN IT. WHY HAVE YOU HANDCUFFED ME?" My throat filled up upon realising that whatever happened had happened for real. I started crying maniacally. After I reclaimed my senses, I explained to them what had happened and that I was not the one they should be restraining. They told me that they had already gone through the security camera footage and they knew that I was not the culprit, and a manhunt was on.

I saw the footage, it was shortly after I walked out of the house, a man with a black jacket and a cap strategically kept at an angle to hide his face, and after 30 minutes, he left in a hurry, trying to cover his face from the camera. It was at that moment that I saw a black spot on the back of his left hand that looked like a wart or a mole. "This, what is this? Are you seeing this?" I pointed at the black spot and appealed to the officers to understand and help me. "We see it, sir, but it's not clear. It can be an injury mark, a blood spot or even a tattoo. And the shape is also not very clear. It's not enough to start investigating. We tried talking to the neighbours, but no one heard a thing.

I stood up and came close to Chaurasiya, "No one heard anything! None? SHE WAS OPENED UP FROM HER CHEST, and you are telling me no one heard anything?" I grabbed his collar. His expression told me something I already knew, "Sir, it seems she was gagged while she was being raped, as we have found samples of forced intercourse, but no semen samples. I wanted this to get over and tried to vent off my anger by hurting him, but was subdued by a tranquilliser.

This was the last time I recognised myself. Since then I have tried everything, every approach to bring someone in. Hiring a private investigator, investigating it myself, and trying to frame someone wrongly just to evade my guilt. Hell, I even tried ending my life! But nothing worked. She was raped and brutally murdered and none of the legal and law protection services were able to help me. My life was in total loss. I have already lost work; my behaviour has become erratic and irrational. I tried finding solace in drowning myself in alcohol, but even that did not work. I tried enforcing a thorough probe through the courts. But this case had become a glory hole, with no stone unturned and still no one to blame.

It took me a year to make my peace with the fact that this is a never-ending battle that I have to fight alone. But then you sent me to Sarvadaman! He did exactly what I was supposed to do. He did justice to his wife. He did the right thing. I tried my best to prove him mentally unstable but that moron accepted all his charges and pleaded guilty in front of the judge. I felt that it was my fault that I could not save him. He did exactly what I should have done. I should not have left Aditi that day. I should have been there and held her hand and said that everything would be alright and that I was with you. It's okay, we will leave this city and go somewhere else, where no one will find you, and I will keep her safe from every threat. And that she is not alone in this, she doesn't have to face all this alone. But instead, I did everything the opposite. I left her alone, I did not listen to her, I doubted her, I thought I was the one suffering equally if not more than her. Then I failed Sarvadaman, who actually did something for his beloved. I am a total failure. I always let down people who counted on me."

"But why did you kill the nurse?" the man with a heavy voice spoke. "You remember when I was admitted to the hospital after being rescued from Dr. Rebellow's basement? I was unconscious for months, with partial episodes of consciousness?" the man nodded. "During that time, sometimes when I woke up, I used to see nurses checking on me, taking my vitals, changing my bed sheet when I had soiled it. Sometimes changing IV.

On one such day, when the nurse was changing my sheet, I was conscious but frail. I saw her taking my sheets. After a short while, she entered my room with a doctor who was trying to get me to respond, but I sank back to sleep. But the very next moment, I saw the same doctor sitting on the sofa in my room, with his pants off, and the same nurse stroking his meat between his legs with her mouth. My ears were ringing, but still, I could hear her slurping over the sausage, and the doctor was really enjoying himself. It was nighttime, and they probably thought I was out cold. She then gradually stood and said, "My turn!" to the doctor. They displaced each other.

The doctor got on his knees and put his head under her skirt. I could see her head drop backwards on the sofa. He then pulled her underpants and flung them away. Then I saw a weird movement as if he was sucking on something, but I was not sure as my vision was coming and going. Suddenly, he said to the nurse, "C'mon, take it off!" commanding her to remove her uniform, which she did at once. That was when I saw a perfect female body which that doctor threw on the sofa, with a firm chest and tight flat belly, but with a penis! The doctor started stroking it, and the nurse kept gasping deeply. They then made their way by sniffing, licking, and inserting each other's rears, which, by the way, both of them were enjoying thoroughly. Their bit each other and his licking her chest and sucking on her sausage, then releasing his juices in her rear, then switching roles. It makes me sick! But it was not the first time they would have done it and was surely not the last. The day Vrinda came to see me with Satya, the same nurse came in to check on me. It was none other than Anupama. At first, I was confused and doubted myself, but as she approached me with familiarity, it was clear as day that it was her. She introduced herself again, and we sat chatting about how hard it was for her to leave the centre, as she had dedicated four years of her life to that NGO, and how Aditi was so kind to take her in and under her wing when she needed a job.

Everyone was just trying to take advantage of her. Then she pursued her nursing course and had been working here, and she was really broken to hear about Aditi's demise and did not have the heart to come see me. She asked me how I ended up here and how I was dealing with such a huge loss. I told her everything that I just told you. I felt a warmth in talking to her as she was close to Aditi, and in a long time, I could remember meeting anyone close to Aditi.

It was her time to check if the bathroom needed cleaning and return to her duties. She opened the door of the bathroom while holding the frame of the door, it was when the warmth was sucked into a cold void that I saw a black spot on the back of her left hand. Everything came rushing to me, like pieces of a jigsaw puzzle falling into place, revealing the big picture.

It was her, Anupama! Who visited Aditi on that fateful day and killed her? And not only Aditi, but she had killed all those poor boys from her NGO. I could not think of anything else, and I walked up to her and smashed her head into the mirror above the basin, as I closed the door behind her. The glass shattered and she fell to the floor, hitting her head on the basin. "What happened, Sir? Why are you doing this?" she asked me while trying to evade me by dragging herself back and still fixating her eyes on me. "Why? Why did you kill Aditi? And those boys?" I asked her. She kept denying the fact that she didn't know about any of this, and what I said made no sense to her, and that she had no motive to harm them or Aditi, and kept begging me to let her go. It was not until I told her that I had seen this black disgusting mark of her's in the security footage. She tried to get back up and tackle me, but I held her by her neck and pushed her face under the water in the toilet pot and held it there till she gave up fighting. She was on the floor, hyperventilating. She is the only person whom I hate the most in this world.

The sweat and water droplets trickled down her face through her throat till they vanished into the canyon between her perfectly round and lifted chest. I had not been with any woman since Aditi, and coming this close to one made me aroused, and I had already left my human side outside when I walked in that door. I leapt onto her, tearing apart her blouse and exposing her chest. I started sucking on the pink patches, and every time I looked at her, I found myself disgusted so I kept one of my hands on her face to cover it.

Once I was done sucking on them, I saw they were swollen and bloody. I quickly dropped my diapers shoved my tool in her mouth and kept stroking her face till I pumped it with my water in it. I sat on the floor as she threw up in the pot. "This is what everyone wanted from me. This very thing! Even men of my own family, in which I was born. Right from my childhood, I had seen the true nature of men, a sexual predator. My father used to hit my mother and then have intercourse with her while she used to cry over the wounds.

When I grew old, he started treating me the same. I didn't choose to be like this; I was born like this. It's not my fault if God made me what I was. Then why was I being subjected to punishment? Why?" She kept crying for a few moments before continuing. "But this partial male hormone gave me the strength of a man in a woman's body.

One night, when my father came home drunk and tried to force himself on me, I pretended to take charge like a dominatrix. I sat on top of him. But I, too, wanted the pleasure that he was feeling, so I tried to enter his rear. But he resisted. But from what I have learnt, resistance can be overcome by force. I made a fist with both my palms and banged his chest. For a few seconds, he was not able to move or breathe. I enjoyed his helplessness. I hit him once again, and again, and one more time, and then kept pounding his chest till his ribs broke and tore his flesh and came out exposing his insides. Then I entered his rear and kept humping him till I was done. That was the first time I felt alive; I felt like I mattered.

The pleasure of making love was not alien to me anymore. But after this, I had to run. My mother covered it up and sent me off on one condition—never to return. From there, I came to Delhi. I did odd jobs sometimes in exchange for money, sometimes in exchange for physical pleasure. But every time anyone saw me naked, they were disgusted by me. I never felt loved. That's all I have ever wanted. But before that, I learnt the hunger of the body.

It was then that I reached Aditi Madam. She was the kindest-hearted person I've ever met. She understood me; she understood it was not my fault for the way I was built. She took me in and kept me close. I started loving her. I wanted to be with her. But I could not risk losing her after expressing my feelings. So I started luring boys, addicted to alcohol. I used to offer them alcohol in exchange for physical pleasure, mine and theirs both. But every time I came on top of them, it reminded me of the high I got when I saw my father dying. I wanted to feel that again, so I bashed their chests with my bare hands. I realised that when the body is in such extreme stress and pain, I bashed their chests with my bare hands and suffocated, men ejaculate.

Then I used their juices, put them on a condom, and made love to them. I always made sure that I had protection with me, and I wore gloves while doing this. Then I used to wipe their bodies with a wet cloth in order to wipe off all my prints." I interjected, "But why, Aditi? What did she do to you?"

She continued. "On the initial days of my recruitment, once I saw her from the crack between the doors of her room. She had just come out of her bath and was standing there without anything on. I realised what those men saw in me. I wanted her, all of her, every inch of her. But she was scared to lose her friendship. But then you came and claimed my territory. I heard the whole action of that night, and I kept jerking myself off listening to the two of you.

When I found it was not enough, I went back to my old way. The next day brought me close to being caught, so I pretended to leave, and I knew you were suspecting a man because of the sexual assault angle. It made it easier to hide in the shadows and follow her. In the mall, in her office back at the centre, I heard that evening when she came back from shopping. Her skin is soft, I must say." It infuriated me as she talked about Aditi. I sprang up and put my foot on her throat and pressed till I heard her bones break. When I lifted my foot, she fell to the side and started crawling towards the door. It was then I picked up a big shard of glass and stabbed her. She twisted with pain. Somehow, I liked it. I stabbed her again, she twisted again, and this continued till the hospital staff broke in."

"So you took your revenge. What did it bring you? Did it bring Aditi back?" The man with a white beard spoke in his usual heavy voice. He got up, infuriated, and started to leave. I said, "Sir, when you have been through the pain that breaks your mind. All it takes is a crack in the glass to shatter. Just like a drop of blood that fell on the ground and gave birth to a similar demon. A drop of blood, a crack in glass. It's the same thing."